# Laundry Day

by Maurie J. Manning

CLARION BOOKS • Houghton Mifflin Harcourt • Boston  New York

# CLARION BOOKS

3 Park Avenue, New York, New York 10016

Copyright © 2012 by

## Maurie J. Manning

FOR INFORMATION ABOUT PERMISSION TO
REPRODUCE SELECTIONS FROM
THIS BOOK, WRITE TO:
PERMISSIONS
HOUGHTON MIFFLIN HARCOURT
PUBLISHING COMPANY
3 Park Avenue
New York, New York 10016

**CLARION BOOKS**
**is an imprint of Houghton Mifflin Harcourt Publishing Company.**

☞ **WWW.HMHBOOKS.COM** ☜

Library of Congress Cataloging-in-Publication Data
Manning, Maurie. ❧ Laundry day / by Maurie J. Manning. ❧ p. cm.
Summary: A boy travels throughout his lively neighborhood, searching for the owner of a red cloth he has found.
ISBN 978-0-547-24196-8
Special Markets ISBN:978-1-328-49237-1
021825.6K1/B1166/A6
[1. Lost and found possessions—Fiction. 2. City and town life—Fiction.] I. Title.
PZ7.M315615Lau 2012
[E]—dc22      2010043252

Manufactured in China ❧ LEO 10 9 8 7 6 5 4 3 2 1
4500678209

Please take mooncake for your help, little boy.

Very tall man at other end of clothesline hang red **nèi yī** to dry. Maybe cloth belong to him.

Now, what would I do with a blanket this small?

Thanks for grabbing my hat, sonny! Maybe the blanket belongs over yonder, to the noisy little fella who's howlin' all the time.

Maybe the organ grinder will play him a lullaby.

What a good idea. Here—a penny for you and a penny for Mr. Travaglini.

Hello, sir. Is this your shawl?

No, my prayer shawls are blue and white. But a nice **fartekh** it would have made for my wife.

Miss, I asked the rabbi and his wife, the girl beating the rug, the four sisters, the organ grinder, the mother with the baby, the prospector, and the laundry lady, but no one has lost this cloth. Can you tell me whose it is?

My birds and I have been watching you all afternoon, **irie** child, and hoping you would find your way to me. That cloth is my beautiful headscarf, which I lost this windy laundry day.

I be thanking you, child. But now you must hurry back down to the street. It's starting to get dark, and your maddah will worry.

Goodbye!